Don't count the number of birthdays.
Count how happy you feel. I'm Birthday
Bear, and I'll help make your birthdays
the best ever.

I'm Wish Bear, and if
you wish on my star,
maybe your special dream
will come true.

If you're ever feeling lonely,
just call on me, Friend Bear.
See, I've got a daisy for you
and a daisy for me.

Grr! I'm Grumpy Bear. There's a cloud on
my tummy to show that I take the grouchies
away, so you can be happy again.

I'm Love-a-Lot Bear. I have two
hearts on my tummy. One is for you;
the other is for someone you love.

It's my job to bring you sweet dreams.
I'm Bedtime Bear, and right now I'm a bit
sleepy. Are you sleepy, too?

Now that you know all of us, we hope
that you'll have a special place for us in your
heart, just like we do for you.

With love from all of us,

The Care Bears

Published in the United States by Parker Brothers, Division of CPG Products Corp.

Care Bears, Care Bears Logo, Tenderheart Bear, Friend Bear, Grumpy Bear, Birthday Bear, Cheer Bear, Bedtime Bear, Funshine Bear, Love-a-Lot
Bear, Wish Bear and Good Luck Bear are trademarks of American Greetings Corporation, Parker Brothers, authorized user.

Library of Congress Cataloging in Publication Data: Wills, Geoffrey. A friend for Frances. SUMMARY: New at school and wishing for
a friend in the third grade, Frances is advised by three "Care Bears."
[1. School stories. 2. Friendship—Fiction] I. Cooke, Tom, ill.
II. Title. PZ7.W68387Fr 1982 [E] 83-2235 ISBN 0-910313-04-0
Manufactured in the United States of America   6 7 8 9 0

A Tale from the
Care Bears

A Friend for Frances

Story by Geoffrey Wills
Pictures by Tom Cooke

It was hot. It felt like summer to Frances, but it was really fall; September, time for a new school year to begin.

At breakfast Frances' mother asked, "Would you like me to drive you to school today?"

"No thanks, Mom," Frances answered.

Frances thought to herself, "I think I am grown up enough to go by myself. After all, I am in the third grade!"

Frances kissed her mother and left for the bus stop.

Since it was her first day at a new school, Frances had to admit to herself that she was feeling a little shy. What if no one spoke to her? "I hope I'm not the only new girl in the third grade," she said to herself. "I hope I am lucky enough to make a new friend."

Suddenly Frances heard a merry voice:
"Good luck, you know, is all around.
Look for it well, and it can be found."
Frances spun around and there, leaning up against
the bus stop sign, was a little, green Bear with a
four-leaf clover on its tummy.

The Bear grinned and spoke.
"I'm one of the Care Bears. Good Luck is my name.
You haven't found luck yet; I think it's a shame.
So I'll give you this clover; its color is green.
Its four leaves bring luck—you'll see what I mean."
"You mean that I might really have good luck
today?" asked Frances.

Good Luck Bear answered:
"That's just what I mean.
Your wish can come true
Good Luck can be yours,
But it's all up to you!"
The bus drew up to the stop and Frances got on.
She turned to wave to Good Luck Bear, but he had
disappeared.

Everyone on the bus seemed to know
everyone else, so Frances took a seat by
herself. "No one seems to notice that I'm
here," Frances thought glumly. "I'll bet
third grade is going to be terrible.
The work will be hard, and the
teacher will be mean. I'm not lucky
at all. I must have imagined that
Good Luck Bear."

But when Frances looked
in her pocket, she still had
the lucky, green clover.

At school Frances walked down the hall to her new classroom. She remembered her old school and all her old friends. Frances suddenly wanted to be back there where she felt safe and comfortable.

Frances sat down and noticed a girl who wore a pretty purple dress. Purple was Frances' favorite color. Frances also saw that the girl wore lovely silver earrings. Frances wished she owned earrings like those.

The girl noticed Frances staring at her and stared back. Frances felt shy and looked away.

Mrs. Rose, the teacher, came in. She welcomed the class, asked everybody to sit down, and began to take attendance. Whenever Mrs. Rose called a name, one of the other students would have something to say.

"Bobby Kelly."

"Hey Bobby, how'd you get your broken arm?"

"Cathy Lee."

"Cathy likes Tommy."

But when Mrs. Rose called Frances' name, no one said anything. Frances answered, "Here," in a small voice. She felt all alone.

Then Mrs. Rose called, "Holly Pepper," and the
girl with the beautiful purple dress answered,
"Present."

Frances thought, "What a beautiful name. Holly
must be the most popular girl in the class." Frances
was thinking so hard that she didn't realize that
the room was silent after Holly's name had been
called too.

Mrs. Rose asked the class to write a story about summer, and as Frances started to write, she heard a strange sound.

"Psst! Frances! Look over here," said a soft furry voice.

Frances looked toward the sound. Outside the classroom window was a little Bear with a shooting star on its tummy.

"It's me, Wish Bear. Good Luck Bear told me about your wish. I've come from Care-a-lot to give you some good advice. Remember this: If you forget your own troubles and think about others, your wish will come true. I'm an expert on wishes, so just remember what I say."

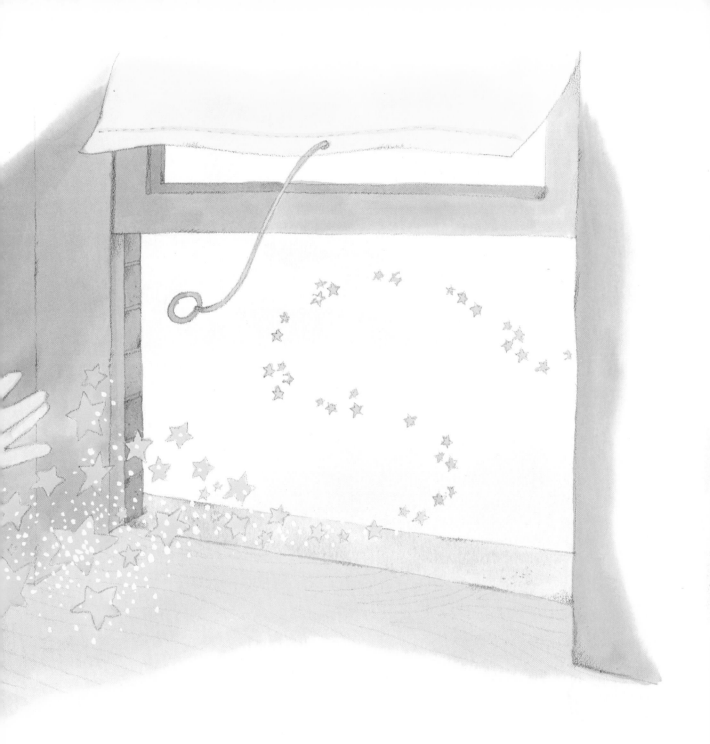

Frances blinked her eyes. Could there really be a
Bear outside the window? When she blinked again,
the Bear was gone, leaving behind a trail of stardust.

The morning passed, and then it was time for lunch. Frances worried as the class walked in line to the lunchroom. Would anyone sit with her?

In the lunchroom, the kids sat in groups. Frances saw that there was no room for her at the first table, so she took a seat at the next one. She opened her lunch box and began to eat. Frances noticed Holly sitting at a nearby table. Holly's lunch box had a pretty rainbow on the front

Then a bunch of boys sat down at the table where Holly was sitting.

Eric looked at Holly and said, "Yuck."

"This is our place. We always sit here," Lou added.

"It's a free country," Holly answered. "I'm new, and I didn't know that this was *your* table." Holly picked up her lunch box and walked away.

Frances was so surprised. She hadn't realized Holly
was a new girl too. Maybe she should have sat next to
her. Oh well, it was too late now. Lunch would soon
be over.

The afternoon passed quickly, and soon it was
time to go home. Frances was glad to get to her house.
She made a snack and went out into the yard. The
day had been hard for her, but she knew that it had
been for Holly, too.

From the shadows behind a tree she heard a gentle voice say, "I think that you are on the right track, Frances. Think about how Holly must be feeling right now." Before she knew it, Frances was joined by a light brown Bear with a big heart on its tummy.

"Which one are you?" Frances asked.
"I'm Tenderheart Bear. I like to help people be nice to each other, so that love can spread and grow."

"I wanted to be nice," Frances said. "But no one talked to me. I was all alone and wished that someone would notice me. I felt awful.

I think *everyone* must have noticed Holly. She was wearing a beautiful dress and had silver earrings."

Tenderheart took Frances by the hand. "Is that how you really feel about Holly? Do you think she is any happier than you are right now?"

"I guess not," Frances admitted. "She's a new girl too."

Tenderheart answered, "Why don't you see if the two new girls can start being friends tomorrow? Holly needs a friend just as much as you do." Then Tenderheart scampered back behind a tree and was gone.

The next morning at school Frances' class had
gym. Everyone ran outside to the playing field. "This
will be a good chance to talk to Holly," Frances
thought.

The class quickly divided into two teams for a relay race. The rules were easy. Touch the base at one end of the course and pass the stick at the other. Frances was excited because she knew that she could run fast. One . . . Two . . . Three, Go!

The first girl on Frances' team was slow. Her team began to lose. Everyone was yelling. Finally only Frances and Holly were left to run for the two teams. Frances ran as fast as she could, but Holly made it back first. Frances' team lost.

Frances felt miserable. Holly's team was giving her a cheer, but Frances' team seemed angry that they had lost, and they just looked at Frances as if she had done something stupid. Now Holly would have lots of new friends, Frances thought, and she would have none.

After gym Frances walked back to the classroom alone. As she sat down at her desk she tried to believe what the Care Bears had told her, but it seemed very hard.

The rest of the class came in, and Holly walked right over to Frances and stood next to her. "You are a good runner," Holly said.

Frances started to look away, but remembered the
big red heart on Tenderheart's tummy. She turned
toward Holly. "You're a good runner, too. Your team
won."

"But you ran fast," Holly said. "Our team was
ahead from the start. That's why we won. I had too
big a lead. This school is full of slowpokes, except for
you. My old school was better."

"Mine, too," Frances said. "I loved gym class at my old school. I miss playing with my friends."

"Me, too," Holly agreed. "Guess what? At my old school my best friend was Frances. Just like your name."

Frances thought for a minute. "If I become your new friend, then you'll have two friends with the same name. It will be the same, but different!"

"Great," said Holly. "I was wishing for a special friend just like the old Frances. Now I have one."

"I wished for a friend, too," said Frances. "Do you want to come over and play at my house tomorrow? We can run races."

On the bus ride home the next day Frances and Holly sat together. Frances felt happy. Her wish had come true. Maybe third grade was not going to be so bad after all.

As the bus slowed down near her stop, Frances thought that she could see three Bears looking out from the bushes and waving to her. She smiled and waved back.

Then she and Holly hopped off the bus and raced home to play together.